The Owlings

THE OWLINGS

D.A. DeWITT

Theolatte
PRESS

To my children
Isaiah, Micah, Josiah,
and Addilynn Joy

CONTENTS

Chapter One

The Thinking Spot

Josiah sat at his window like he did almost every evening. What was he doing, you ask, well, that's a good question. He's thinking. And this is his thinking spot.

Thinking helps him fall asleep, and he always has a lot to think about. He thinks about what happened at school each day. He thinks about what he talked about with his mom over dinner. Sometimes he even thinks about what they had for dinner — as long as it wasn't liver and onions.

Tonight they had goulash, and he really didn't feel like spending much time thinking about goulash. Not because it's just not his favorite, which it isn't, but because dinner wasn't as much fun as it usually was. Josiah's mom has been kind of stressed lately, and their dinner table, which is normally filled with conversation about their day, has been rather quiet lately.

On this night, like most nights, Josiah couldn't help but think about his dad and how much he missed him. His dad passed away nearly two years ago. Josiah would talk with him about all the things he likes to think about. They would sit right at this very spot, by his window. And tonight he's missing their late evening conversations, even more than he usually does.

Dusk is Josiah's favorite time of day. It's when he does his best thinking. He sits with his arms folded over the second story bedroom windowsill, looking across the farmland that his dad inherited from his father who inherited it from his great grandfather before him.

It's a family farm and one day it will belong to Josiah. He thinks about that sometimes, what it will be like to own a farm, and what it will be like to be an adult. On this particular evening there is a dim red hue fading in the sky as he looks across the silhouetted trees in his backyard. Lightning bugs lingering over from the summer months decorate the night sky like shiny polka dots.

Nature is noisy, he thinks to himself. The chirping of the crickets is humming like the sound of a washing machine. And it's one of the years when cicadas, what people often wrongly call locusts, come out and leave their brown shells all over the place. Josiah loves to collect the crunchy molten skins. They look just like the bugs but instead are mere hollow versions left behind. At night, the cicadas make a loud pulsing noise, the kind of sound you might expect in a scary movie when something bad is about to happen.

There's a slight breeze shaking the branches outside his window, keeping a sporadic rhythm. And completing the symphony of sounds is the baritone hoots of the owls, which seem to be coming from some ways away.

On this night, Josiah wished the owls could actually talk instead of merely saying "who, who" over and over again. He's always felt as though their calls kept him company as he sits at his window thinking. But tonight it would be great if they could actually share a conversation. They are, after all, supposed to be really wise.

Sometimes thinking is better when you actually have someone to think with; someone to talk to. It's especially helpful when you have those big questions that make it hard to go to sleep.

And on this night Josiah had a lot of questions.

An interesting thing happened in his science class today. His normal teacher just had a baby and would be out for a while, so they had a new substitute teacher named Sam. Most of the teachers at Josiah's school had you call them by their last name, but not Sam. He was really nice, but Josiah wasn't quite sure what to think about some of the things he said in class.

Sam started the class today by writing the following words on the chalkboard, "Everything was created by nature."

A student raised her hand and asked, "You mean everything?"

"That's right," Sam said. "Nature is all that has or ever will exist. So, everything comes from nature. Does that make sense to you?" Sam asked her.

"I'm not sure," she said.

"Okay, let me try to explain. Everything we see came from nature, even humans. Nature made everything there is."

"But I came from my mom," she quickly responded.

"That's right. But you have to track it all the way to the beginning of time. Your mom came from her mom, and her mom came from her mom. But long ago, before there were humans, nature just moved along slowly until human beings were born. Nature created everything. It is all that exists, so everything comes from it."

"So nature is my great, great, great, great grandparent?" another student blurted out with a bit of a laugh, to which Sam reminded the class that they need to wait their turn before they speak.

This has always been a funny rule to Josiah. *You never see adults raising their hands in adult conversations to see who gets to go next*, he thought to himself.

Sam spent the rest of the hour explaining why people like to think there is something outside of nature. "We want there to be more than nature. Some people like to think that things like fairytales or gods are real," Sam said, "but there simply isn't anything outside of nature. And the more we understand this, the more we will learn to love nature for what it is."

Josiah wasn't sure this statement was true. He liked the idea that there was something more, and yet he still loved nature. He didn't really feel like he had to make a choice between the two.

Alton, the boy who sits next to Josiah, raised his hand and asked a good question, "If there is nothing outside of nature, then where did nature come from?"

Sam tried to help Alton understand how nature had created itself, which seemed quite confusing to everyone in class, including Josiah. But the bell rang before anyone else could assault the substitute teacher with more questions, and for young students there are few things that distract their attention more than the final bell.

Now, here at the end of the day, Josiah sat, looking out of his window, with the country sounds of the night cooing him to sleep. He wondered if his teacher was right, if nature really is all that exists. With questions about nature, and wishful thinking about owls, he closed his eyes and rested his head to one side in the crook of his arm that was still draped across the windowsill.

And this is where our story really begins.

* * *

Peck. Peck. Peck.

Kerplunk.

Josiah abruptly awoke as his arm slipped down to the floor and his head landed with a thud on the frame of the open window. Rubbing his forehead, he looked up to see an owl perched on a tree limb, only inches away from his bedroom window. An owl had never come this close to Josiah before. He quit rubbing his head and started rubbing his eyes. Something seemed really odd about this owl.

The owl was wearing clothes, and not just any clothes, he was wearing some sort of dark dress coat that looked like a cape. He had a tweed vest on over a dress shirt with a funny looking necktie. An eyepiece sat above his beak, covering one eye, with a little gold chain draped down to the side of his head. He was leaning slightly to his left side and seemed to support his weight on a small wooden cane, which had a brass ring at the top.

"How do you do?" The owl said with an odd accent.

Josiah, still rubbing his eyes, quickly crawled backwards away from the window. "This can't be real. This can't be..." he said out loud to himself.

"Alright?" The owl interrupted.

"Wh... Wha... What?" Josiah said with a shaky voice that had just a hint of excited curiosity.

"Are you okay, lad? The name's Gilbert. Delighted to finally make your acquaintance." The owl clumsily extended his wing as if to shake Josiah's hand. I say clumsily because when he did this, he lost the grip on his cane and it fell to the ground below.

Josiah didn't know what to think. *Owls aren't supposed to talk. It's impossible! I must be dreaming*, he thought to himself. And with that last thought, his head became flushed and a crooked smile came over his face. The last thing he remembered the next morning was falling backwards onto his bed.

Chapter Two

The Wooden Cane

Josiah woke up his usual way with his mom turning the hallway light on and opening his door. "Wake up sugar booger," she would always say. That always made Josiah giggle. Moms are good at finding ways to get little boys out of bed.

He sat up, rolled to the side, and put his bare feet down onto the wooden floor; and then suddenly he remembered the owl from the night before. Sitting on the edge of his bed, still a little muddleheaded from just waking up, he concluded that it must have been a dream. He nearly laughed out loud thinking about how funny the owl looked with his cape, tie, and cane. And that accent! *Wow, what a dream*, he thought.

He walked down the stairs, carefully skipping the third step from the bottom because of the way it always creaks if you step on it. He made his way to the kitchen and sat down at their small breakfast table. His mom already had his cereal poured and a big glass of orange juice waiting for him. She was sipping her coffee and looking over the newspaper when he sat down.

"How did you sleep?" she asked, as she continued reading.

"Okay. I had a funny dream though about an owl dressed up like an old man," he said.

"That's nice dear," his mom remarked, while obviously preoccupied by the newspaper.

Josiah wanted to say more about how weird the whole thing with the owl was, and how real it seemed to him at the time, but he could tell he wasn't going to get anywhere with her. She's been pretty distracted the past few weeks. Though she was normally cheerful and funny, lately she's seemed sad.

After Josiah finished breakfast, he got up and gave his mom a big hug.

"What was that for," she asked.

"Nothin'. Love you Mom," Josiah said, as he grabbed his backpack and headed for the door. He walked through his front yard and down to the gravel road that led to the bus stop where his best friend Addi was already waiting.

Addi is the same age as Josiah. They've been friends as long as he can remember. Her family is their closest neighbor. Actually, they were their only neighbors, unless you count the Braleys who lived about a mile away. Josiah and Addi's homes were about five miles out of town. Between the two families they owned a little over two hundred acres of farmland.

Josiah and his mom lived on a smaller plot of land that was long and narrow and stretched along the highway. Addi's house was down the gravel road that turned off the highway. From Josiah's house it was about a five minute walk, or just two minutes if you were riding a bike, or less than a minute if you were riding in a car.

When the weather was bad, Addi's mom would drive her to the bus stop and Josiah would sit with them until the bus came. Addi's mom was nice. Josiah really liked her. And he liked Addi's dad, too. He was some kind of police officer, but he mainly took care of parks and animals. One time he let Josiah ride in his car when he did his morning patrol. He even turned the lights and siren on. That's probably one of the reasons that Josiah, for the present time, wanted to be a police officer when he's an adult. That is if he doesn't make it onto a professional sports team or become the President of the United States.

Josiah liked spending time at Addi's house. Lately, he had spent a lot of time over there, especially when his mom had to work late. Every Wednesday he and his mom would join Addi's family for dinner. They started doing this nearly three years ago after Josiah's dad became sick, and they've been doing it ever since.

Some of the kids at school liked to tease Josiah for being best friends with a girl. Josiah always acted like it didn't bother him, though it really did. But he was glad to have Addi for friend, and unlike the kids at school, she understood him. She knew Josiah's dad before he had passed away. From time to time they would talk about him, which always made Josiah feel a little better on the days when he was feeling kind of low.

Today the weather was nice so Addi had walked to the bus stop. She stood with Josiah next to the yellow bus sign. It was early autumn and the weather was starting to get a little cooler. The trees were just starting to change their colors. The wind carried a crisp chill that let you know fall wasn't too far away.

Josiah loved this time of year. Some of his favorite things have to do with fall: bonfires, hot apple cider, jumping in piles of leaves, trick or treating, and best of all, his birthday was in late October.

The bus pulled to the stop. The brakes on the bus always squeaked loudly. You could always hear the bus slowing down as it came around the corner on the highway. The two of them shuffled up the steep bus steps and to the back left side to their normal seat. Addi always let Josiah sit by the window. She didn't really care whether she was by the window or the aisle, and she knew Josiah like to look out the window while they talked on their way to school.

As soon as they sat down Josiah began telling Addi about his dream. The two of them laughed about the idea of an owl with clothes and a cane.

"I'd like to have a dream like that," Addi said. "Except I would want it to be a talking squirrel."

"Why a squirrel?" Josiah asked with a funny look

on his face.

"Because they're cute," Addi answered, as if that would settle matters.

"I like to eat squirrel," Josiah said. "Especially when your mom cooks it."

Addi's dad liked to hunt and sometimes they would have wild game for dinner. Addi's mom would fry the squirrel meat in a pan with some kind of special sauce that Josiah thought had to be about the best sauce in the world. She knew it was Josiah's favorite so she would make it on a regular basis.

"Not me, I think it's gross," Addi exclaimed. "You shouldn't eat squirrels. They're cute!" She demanded.

Josiah gave Addi a hard time about the idea of talking squirrels, but she of course just returned fire by teasing him about talking owls that wore clothes.

They could have fun like this without making each other mad (most of the time, at least). And after all they both liked stories of talking animals, especially ones that involved children visiting new worlds. Some of their favorite stories were about these very things. But they didn't have time to think about different worlds, or even talking animals.

The bus had stopped at the school and they had to hustle or they wouldn't make it to class before the first bell rang. Sometimes the bus ran a little late, and today was just one of those days. They dashed into the school building, made a quick stop by their lockers, grabbed a drink from the water fountain, and made it to their desks just in time.

Their first class was math. Josiah felt like there weren't enough erasers in the world to get him through math class. He was always making mistakes and needing to erase his work and start all over. Math was far from his favorite subject. But Addi, on the other hand, she was a math wiz, but she didn't rub that in Josiah's face. She would always help him on his math homework when he would get stuck from time to time.

Their third class of the day was art and that had to be one of Josiah's best classes. His teacher's name was Mrs. Long, and he thought she was about the nicest person he had ever met. Some teachers would let students pick on each other, but not Mrs. Long. In her class you knew you were safe. And not only that, but Josiah loved to draw. He would lose track of time in her class. Today he tried drawing the owl from his dream, which made Addi laugh. So, she worked on a sketch of a talking squirrel, but she didn't get too far before she gave up. She wasn't nearly as good as him.

Their last class of the day was science where Sam, the substitute teacher, welcomed the class and started his lesson. Usually Josiah had to work at being alert and attentive late in the afternoon, but after the discussion in yesterday's class, he was curious to see what they would talk about today.

"Some of you had questions about what we talked about yesterday," Sam said, "so I thought I would try to clear things up a little today.

"Nature is all that has ever existed. Billions of years

ago, we're not sure how long exactly, the natural world exploded into existence."

"It exploded," someone asked.

"Please remember to raise your hand," Sam reminded them. "Yes, it exploded. Scientists call it the Big Bang."

"What made it explode?" Alton asked after Sam called on him. Alton liked to ask a lot of questions.

"That's a really good question," the teacher said. "We think nature either came out of nothing, or at least very little. It's something that scientist call the quantum vacuum. Okay, Alton, you could put your hand down. I think I know what you are going to ask. It isn't that kind of vacuum, like a vacuum cleaner that you have at your house," Sam said.

Alton put his hand down. Obviously Sam was right about his question.

The teacher continued, "The quantum vacuum has been described as 'nothing' by some scientists. And they think it could have created everything."

Daniel, a student who sits on the other side of the classroom from Josiah, raised his hand. "Yes, Daniel," Sam said. "What's your question?"

"You mean nothing created nature?"

"Well, sort of. Yes. We're not really sure. But what we are fairly confident about is that nature is all there is, so it either has always existed or it somehow came from nothing," replied Sam.

The class continued to ask questions, and Sam patiently tried to respond to each one, but then the final bell rang, which is the sound of freedom to every schoolboy and schoolgirl. It was like the running of the bulls. Josiah was just thankful he didn't get trampled.

Josiah got out from behind his desk and stretched his legs. He let out a loud yawn, which got the attention of his teacher. Sam looked up with a smile and asked, "Did I bore you today?"

"Oh, no," Josiah said through another yawn. "I'm just sleepy."

"Did you not get enough sleep?" Sam asked.

Josiah told him he was up late and had a weird dream, but he didn't have time to talk about the details with his substitute teacher. He barely had enough time to make it to down the hall to the bathroom, then to his locker, then out to the bus before the bus driver, who always seemed like he was in a hurry, pulled out of the parking lot. So Josiah simply thanked his teacher as he ran out into the hallway.

When Josiah and Addi got off the bus that afternoon, they said their normal goodbyes and headed towards their separate houses, Addi down the gravel road and Josiah through his front yard. As he made his way to the front door he could see that he had left his bedroom window wide open. His mom would always get on to him for that because it let bugs get in. This year there were a lot of stinkbugs for some reason, and Josiah was certain he would find a bunch of them in his room now.

Instead of walking immediately to the door, he went over beneath his window and looked up as he contemplated the trouble it was going to be to chase all of the stinkbugs out the house—and the horrid smell he would have to deal with if he squashed them.

If you don't know what stinkbugs are, they're ugly little insects that are kind of flat and wide and have a pointy little face. And they let out a weird smell if you smash them. Josiah hated that smell.

As he stood under the pine tree beneath his second story window his foot hit something and he nearly tripped over it. He looked down to investigate and saw what looked like a really smooth stick partially covered up in pine needles. He knelt down and swept the needles off to discover a wooden cane. Josiah quickly held it up to examine it more closely.

It was about eighteen inches long. It looked like it was made of oak. It had an aged brass ring at the top with the name Gilbert stamped, or carved, it was hard to tell, on the bottom.

A thought occurred to Josiah that this looked like, but surely couldn't be, the owl's cane from the night before.

But it couldn't be... it just couldn't be, Josiah thought to himself. *Last night was a dream. This couldn't belong to the owl. It just couldn't.*

* * *

That evening Josiah's mom made his favorite meal, spaghetti and meatballs. His mom's grandparents were originally from Italy, so anytime she cooked Italian food it was always amazing. She would bake the meatballs in the oven, then let them simmer in the sauce on the stove. She would always make garlic bread to go with the spaghetti. The smells filled their house and made Josiah nearly forget all about the cane that he had put under his pillow upstairs.

Since he lost his father, their home seemed to always be missing something. Sometimes it felt empty. But there were times when his mom cooked Italian food, with all of the smells of garlic and meatballs and pasta, that made him feel like his dad was just in the other room, relaxing on the couch, waiting for dinner to be ready. That's one of the reasons why Josiah likes spaghetti and meatballs so much. It's the kind of food that brings back good memories.

When they sat down to eat, his mom still looked sad. Her face had the telltale signs of tears. Josiah asked her what was wrong. She reassured him that everything was okay. She said they had some things to talk about, but it could wait for another time.

He could tell she made a decision, that very instant, to smile, and to look happy. She brushed her hair to one side, propped her arm on the table, rested her head on her hand, and said, "How was your day, pumpkin?"

She called him that sometimes too. Maybe he was getting a little too old for cutesy nicknames, but when she called him that it made him feel good inside, as if everything was all right. Josiah liked getting older, and wanted to be older, but sometimes, didn't mind things that made him still feel little.

He began telling her all about his day, and just like

old times, they sat at the table for a long time talking. After they had shared a plate of no bake cookies, his favorite dessert, and a couple glasses of milk, he began to tell her about his dream of the talking owl. But before he got a chance to tell her about the cane, his mom told him it was time to head upstairs and get ready for bed.

That evening Josiah sat by his window waiting and hoping the owl would come back. He finally propped his pillow on the windowsill, wrapped his blanket around him, and got more comfortable as he prepared to sit as long as it might take until the owl returned. He stood the cane upright on the windowsill, leaning to one side. And he waited.

The wind howled in the trees that night. There was no rain, but you would have thought a thunderstorm was about to break out any minute. Josiah reluctantly drifted to sleep, more than a little disappointed about not seeing the owl. This seemed to prove that the other night must have been a dream. He was fairly certain now, though he didn't know where the little cane came from. His best bet for seeing the owl again would be in his dreams.

Chapter Three

Bad News and a Scary Owl

Wednesday morning rushed in with a surprise. The wind must have caused a power outage that night because none of the alarm clocks in the house were working. Josiah's mom scuttled into his room and found him sleeping on the floor. "Get up honey, we overslept!" Josiah jumped up and threw on an outfit his mom had quickly set out for him.

Before leaving his room, he picked up the blanket and pillow by the window to put them away. And that's when he noticed it… the cane was gone.

Josiah looked out the window to see if it had fallen back beneath the pine tree. No sign of it. He looked under his bed and under his dresser. Nothing. He yelled downstairs to his mom to ask if she had seen a cane.

"What?" she asked. "Honey, we really don't have time for..." Her comment was interrupted by a persistent, but light, knocking at the door. She opened the door to discover Addi who blurted out, in quite an anxious and excited tone, that she had told the bus driver, who always seemed like he was in a hurry, to wait just a minute so she could try to get Josiah.

Josiah ran down the stairs, accidentally stepping on the third step from the bottom, which he generally tried to avoid because of the loud creak it always made. He grabbed a poptart to eat on the way to school, gave his mom a hug, and, along with Addi, hustled off to the bus.

Without hesitation Addi asked him if he dreamed of talking owls again as they got situated in their bus seat. Josiah told her all about the cane and the two of them got that weird, eerie, exciting feeling, like you get when something really cool, or kind of scary is about to happen.

"Do you think the owl came back to take the cane?" Addi asked.

"I don't know what to think. Maybe I imagined the cane too," he said.

"But how could you imagine it when you found it in the middle of the day?" she asked.

"I know. I know. It doesn't make sense. Maybe the cane was just a coincidence. I mean, I can't be certain the cane I found was the same one the owl was holding. And maybe the cane just fell out of the window last night. Maybe I'll be able to find it when I get home."

"That's a lot of maybes," Addi said.

"I know. Maybe the owl was real," Josiah said.

"That version doesn't seem to need as many maybes," Addi said with a laugh.

"I can't argue with that," replied Josiah.

"So, how are your talking squirrels?" Josiah added. He couldn't resist.

And with that, Addi punched him in the arm.

When they got to school, the bus driver grumpily told everyone it was time to get off the bus. He always said that. Josiah wasn't sure why. It seemed rather obvious that when the bus stopped in the school parking lot it was time to get out. *And what do school bus drivers do all day long between their morning pick-ups and their afternoon drop-offs,* Josiah wondered.

They all piled off the bus in a line like little penguins and then dispersed, going mostly different directions once they entered the school building. Except for Josiah and Addi. They stuck together as usual. They stopped by their lockers, grabbed their stuff, and then stood around for about five minutes or so before class began.

The bus had been a little early that morning which always meant an awkward gap of time between getting to school and then trying to look happily engaged in social activities until the first bell rang. The important thing was to look occupied. The worst thing would be to look lost or lonely. *Maybe this was the sort of thing that gets easier as you get older,* Josiah thought. He really didn't care for standing around the hallways trying to look important.

The bell rang soon enough, to Josiah's relief, and then he was faced with another challenge. Math. So he got out his pencil and erasers and prepared to defeat his numerical foes one at a time. He couldn't let one class ruin his perfectly good report card. And with Addi's help later, he would figure out anything he might get stuck on in the day's lesson.

At lunchtime, Josiah waited in line in the cafeteria. Normally he brought his lunch, but since he and his mom overslept, he was forced to eat a soupy brown entrée spread over pasta that was said to be beef and noodles. Nothing about the presentation or the smell excited his appetite. Addi was kind enough to give him half of her peanut butter sandwich. While most people like peanut butter and jelly together, Addi preferred her PB&J without the J. They also split an apple. Before long, the bell rang and it was time to head back to class.

The afternoon rolled on at a humdrum pace, punctuated by the ringing of bells all the way through the final bell of the day at the end of science class. Though the last couple of days in science were filled with an air of controversy and confusion, today was pretty bland. He and Addi headed to the bus, where the driver, again, as usual, was in a hurry. He waited for them with a lackluster expression as though they were not moving quickly enough. Josiah wondered what he had been up to all day.

When they got to their bus stop they walked straight to Josiah's front yard. On Wednesdays they would normally head to Addi's house immediately since this is the day of the week their families always shared dinner. But all they could talk about on the bus ride home was the cane that Josiah found the day before, and that it was missing when he woke up this morning. They were determined to see if it had indeed simply fallen out of the window while he was sleeping.

But their search was in vain. Together they strolled to Addi's house with the excitement of the thought that the talking owl, with the funny clothes and the odd accent, might actually be real. Maybe he had come back for his cane last night, they mused. It was like a whole other world had opened up before their eyes; but it wasn't a different world like they had read about in the stories where children find a passage into another place. It was like they had found a secret door into their own world.

They knew they couldn't tell their parents, because adults don't usually take this kind of thing seriously. And besides, even if they were wrong, the idea that owls really could talk was enough to stir their enthusiasm. They wanted to bask in their imagination. They walked into Addi's house trying to conceal their excitement. They planned to get out the art supplies and make another picture of the owl.

But a cold mood, like a dark cloud, met them at the door.

Addi's parents and Josiah's mom were sitting around the dinner table. It was a little early for dinner so there was no food sitting out. And there were none of the pleasant smells of food simmering in the kitchen like there normally would be on Wednesday afternoons. Both moms looked like they were crying. Addi's dad looked upset as well.

The children froze in the doorway. They knew something wasn't right. Something serious. Something that would change their lives.

They walked towards the basement hoping to escape whatever it was, but their parents asked them to come sit at the table. The walk from the front door to the dining room seemed like a country mile. And this is when Josiah began to understand what had been troubling his mom.

Addi's dad led the conversation. He told them about the recent plans their state government had made to improve transportation between two cities, one about two hours south of their home and the little town just north of them where they went to school. Josiah and Addi had both heard adults talking about the interstate, but they didn't understand what this had to do with them or their parents.

"The highway next to your house, Josiah, is going to be turned into one of the lanes of the interstate," he told them.

"Oh. Cool. Where will the other lane go?" Josiah asked.

Addi's father looked down at the floor and then at Josiah. With a serious, but compassionate look on his face, he explained that the interstate lanes would be much wider and require much more land than the current highway. There would be a median in the middle of the lanes and large shoulders along the sides of the interstate. It would require a lot of land.

And this, Josiah learned, meant their family farm land. And that's when he learned the worst news of all, the second lane of the interstate would be built even further over and would run where their house is located. So much land from their farm was needed for the interstate, the government claimed the entire farm. Addi's house was just outside of the plot required for the interstate development, so their farm would be left alone, except for one small stretch of land on their border.

"So, what's going to happen to our house?" Josiah asked, turning to his mom.

Her eyes filled with tears as she looked at Josiah. "They will have to tear it down." She answered. She pulled her chair over to Josiah and pulled him even closer to her. She wrapped him in her arms and began sobbing quietly.

Josiah lightly pushed back and said, "But I don't want them to tear our house down!"

Addi's dad placed his hand on Josiah's shoulder and tried to explain to him that they had no choice. The government had the right to demand their land. It was something called eminent domain. There was nothing they could do about it.

Josiah got up from the table and walked out onto the front porch; his mom following closely behind. They sat on the porch swing for several minutes before either of them spoke. His mom put her arm around him and he leaned his head on her shoulder.

"I don't want to lose our house. It reminds me of Dad. It's all I have left of him," Josiah said, fighting back his tears.

"I know. I know," his mom kept repeating as she squeezed him tighter. "It will all be okay."

"When do we have to move?" Josiah asked.

"This weekend," his mom answered. "I waited as long as I could to tell you. I was hoping," she stopped for a moment to clear her throat. She labored to complete her sentence, "... I was hoping that if I waited maybe something would happen. Maybe we would be able to stay. I'm so sorry, Josiah. I'm so sorry. I don't want this to happen any more than you do."

And with those words the final attempts to hold back their emotions were removed and the two cried together for what seemed to Josiah like a really long time. He still had a lot of questions but remained silent. It just seemed more appropriate.

Nothing else was said until Addi's mom stepped onto the front porch, holding the screen door open, to let them know dinner was on the table. Josiah and his mom slowly walked back into the house, arm in arm. Deli sandwiches and fresh fruit were sitting on the table with several glasses of apple cider. Everyone sat down and looked towards Addi's dad, who nodded as if to say it was okay to begin eating.

Dinner was quiet that evening, as you might expect. Little else was said about the move, except that it became clear, between what little comments were exchanged between the adults, that the plan was for

Josiah and his mom to move into Addi's house on Saturday, and to stay with them until they figured out what to do next.

After dinner, they all sat on the front porch together watching the sunset and listening to the rustling leaves. It was as though the cool breeze was struggling to push back the veil of dark emotions that hung like a lingering storm over Addi's house. It was a clash of hope and despair whirling in the autumn wind.

Josiah felt it, even if no one else did. They all hugged and said their goodbyes and for a moment it seemed as though hope might have the final say, but sadness rejoined them on their short ride home. It seems as though sometimes joy has to simmer for a while before it can rise to the top.

As they walked into the front door, Josiah noticed something he had missed earlier in his rush to make it out to the bus. There was the cane sitting on top of the small dining table in the kitchen. His mom picked it up and handed it to him and asked him where it came from. She said she found it that morning when she came in to wake him up for school.

Josiah explained how he had found it under their pine tree the day before. As he made his way up the steps, he began to realize that the owl must have only been a dream. It had not come back for the cane. So, like the rest of the day, even the excitement of the talking owl with a weird accent, was swept away by the flood of disappointment.

In just two days he would be moving out of the

only home he had ever known. It was the only home his father had ever known, and the only home his grandfather had ever known before him. His great grandfather had built the house years ago.

If the prospects of a talking owl had made things seem to come into full color earlier that afternoon, the events of this evening had brought life back into muted shades of gray.

Josiah didn't sit at his window that night. He flopped down onto his bed, atop of his comforter, and closed his eyes. He was asleep in minutes. The emotions of it all had drained his energy.

But he was awoken suddenly when he heard a tapping noise.

He jumped out of bed and knelt down in front of his window, which was closed. He opened it and looked out with a subdued idea of what he might see. Though at this point he had nearly closed the case on the mysterious owl, and concluded that it was only a dream. But he was still curious.

He didn't see or hear anything for a few moments. He leaned out of the window and looked up in the tree and still saw nothing. *Maybe it was just a branch hitting the window*, he thought to himself.

After a few minutes of looking out across their property, he started to think about the new interstate again. *What would Dad think*, he wondered. He just couldn't accept that this land, and this house, that belonged in their family for so long, would have to be torn down. He would no longer be able to sit at this window, where he used to sit with his dad. He would no longer be able to spend the evening thinking about life, and looking across their family farm.

Just as the emotions welled up again inside of him, Josiah heard the *who* of an owl. And it was really close. Really close. In fact, it was right under his nose. He looked down towards the ground and right below him was an owl perched on a branch. He had missed it because he only looked up and out.

But this was not the owl from his dream, or what he thought was a dream. This owl didn't wear clothes, or carry a cane, or talk. At least it didn't say anything that Josiah could understand. It just *hooed*. It was brown with patches of white speckled across its chest and feathers.

The owl had a mysterious look about him. He swayed from one side to the next while glaring at Josiah with his big round eyes. It was hard to tell if his eyes were inquisitive or fierce. Josiah began to get a sinking feeling that maybe this owl wasn't nice at all. *What if it was mean*, he thought. The two just stared at each other for several minutes.

Finally, Josiah had enough. The way this day had gone, he didn't want to take any chances. He tried to shoo the owl away, but it wouldn't budge.

He whispered at the owl, telling it to go away. It was a forceful whisper, but not too loud as he didn't want to wake up his mother. He told the owl to get. But the owl just moved his head from side to side with his eyes locked on Josiah's. It was if the owl knew something,

something that it wanted to tell Josiah, but couldn't, or wouldn't.

Slowly Josiah became angry at the owl. He wanted him to talk. He wanted talking animals to be real. He wanted something today to be happy and hopeful.

Exasperated, Josiah took a pencil off of his desk and went back to the window and threw it at the owl. The owl dodged the pencil, but stayed on the branch. Josiah didn't want to hurt it, he just wanted it to fly away. But it wouldn't. It kept hooting louder and louder. Josiah began to feel as though the owl was taunting him.

Josiah wanted to scream, but he knew better. "What?" he said in a muted yell. "What do you want from me? Why can't you just talk? Say something!"

The owl just looked up at him, with its head moving from right to left in a rhythmic motion. Finally, Josiah gave up. He closed his window and got back in his bed. He could hear the owl continue hooting for some time before he drifted back to sleep.

Chapter Four

Calzones and a Chocolate Cannoli

It was Thursday morning, and a loud clap of thunder shook the house and woke Josiah. He sat up and looked out the window but all he could see was sheets of rain flowing down the glass pane. He couldn't see out into his yard, it was raining so hard. He thought that this is what it must look like for a fish in an aquarium, trying to look out at the world. He glanced over at the alarm clock just as it began to beep.

Sometimes Josiah would incorporate the beeping sound of the alarm into his dreams. Sometimes he would imagine it was the beeping of a truck backing up. Or if he was having a more exciting dream, the noise from his alarm clock might become the ticking of a time bomb, counting down as he worked to defuse it and save the world.

But not today, he was wide-awake because of the storm. He reached over and turned the alarm clock off. As he got out of bed, he glanced back at the window, thinking of the owl that wouldn't go away or stop hooting, He just shook his head. *Owls*, he thought to himself, *who needs them*.

He made his way downstairs where his mom was making waffles. This was an obvious attempt to cheer him up. He loved waffles, and he loved that his mom wanted to cheer him up. He was still a little numb from all of the news, but he was more concerned about her this morning than he was about himself. That's something he learned from his dad. Josiah was a good son.

His mom stopped what she was doing and walked over next to their breakfast table and gave him a hug. "You doing okay?" she asked. Josiah just nodded and forced a smile as a he looked up at her.

His mom placed a plate of hot waffles in front of him. She walked over and took a small white pitcher filled with syrup out of the microwave. She knew Josiah liked his syrup heated. They enjoyed breakfast together before getting ready to head out into the rain and face the day.

Josiah ran to the bus stop where Addi was sitting in her mom's car. He got in the backseat as he shook the rain out of his hair, which sprayed water over everyone in the front seat.

"Oops, sorry!" he said. Everyone laughed. It was

raining really hard. Addi's mom had to turn on the windshield wipers just so they could see if the bus had pulled up yet. When it did arrive, the two of them ran as fast as they could to avoid getting too wet. Josiah accidentally left his lunch bag in the back seat, which would only mean one thing, he would have to eat cafeteria food again today. He didn't realize he had forgotten it until lunchtime. He stood on his tiptoes in line at the cafeteria, trying to get a peek at what was on the menu. Addi had already offered half of her PB minus the J sandwich. But to his surprise they had cheeseburgers. It's hard to mess up a cheeseburger.

When he finally made it through the line, Addi already had half her sandwich sitting on a napkin waiting for him. They decided to go fifty-fifty, so Josiah kept the sandwich half and gave Addi half of his cheeseburger. That's when Josiah told Addi that his mom had the cane all along. They both shrugged as if it didn't matter, but deep down they really liked the idea of talking owls being real.

The disappointment of finding the cane, coupled with the news of the interstate, was enough to make lunch miserable, but cheeseburgers have a funny way of making things seem better. And besides, neither of them felt like being too serious today.

Their conversation turned to more interesting things, like the new dragon movie that was playing at the drive-in theater that weekend. This was the last weekend the drive-in was open for the season. Come Monday, it would be closed until next summer.

If they played their cards right, they might be able to go on Friday or Saturday night. Addi didn't care for dragons all that much, but she figured there would probably be a princess in the film. *What good is a dragon if there isn't a princess around,* she thought. Later that day they spent their bus ride home devising a plan to get their parents to take them.

When they got off the bus, they stood for a moment looking at Josiah's house. They didn't need to say anything. They both knew. There wouldn't have many more chances like this. Next week the construction would begin to make room for the new highway.

Their trance was broken when Josiah's mom stepped out and waived at them. She walked across the yard to where they were standing. With a smile on her face Josiah's mom asked them, "Do you guys know what's playing at the drive-in this weekend?"

Kids can spot a bribe from a mile away, but neither of them minded one bit. They both knew that this would be the perfect thing to get their minds off of the move. Their faces beamed.

"Would you two like to go?" his mom asked.

"Seriously?" they said in unison.

"Seriously," his mom replied as she walked them into the house. "Addi, your mom is running errands and she is going to pick you up when she gets back." They were greeted by the smell of freshly baked chocolate chip cookies. Josiah's mom poured cold milk into tall glasses and set them on the table.

At this point, the only thing Josiah and Addi wanted

to talk about was the movie. "Are you sure my parents are okay for us to go to the dragon movie?" Addi asked.

"Yep. I've already talked them. We're going to go on Saturday night."

Josiah and Addi looked at each and grinned widely. They loved going to the drive-in. They didn't realize that most towns no longer have drive-in movies. To them this was the normal, and best, way to see a movie. Staying up late, eating popcorn, seeing friends, watching a movie under the stars. It couldn't get much better.

When Addi's mom picked her up, Addi immediately verified that they were all going to the movie. "Are we really going mom?" she asked. "You bet. It's all set!" her mom answered. Josiah and his mom stood on their front porch and waved goodbye as Addi and her mom pulled out of their driveway.

They decided to sit on the front step for a while and just talk. Neither of them really felt like talking about their move. Josiah had gotten past the shock of the news, and he was still upset, but he knew they couldn't change anything.

That's one of the important lessons that he had learned from his dad. His father was a calm and collected person, who rarely got sidetracked by anything. Josiah was a lot like his dad.

"Well, I don't have anything for dinner." His mom said. "I didn't buy many groceries since... " she paused.

"Since we're moving Saturday," Josiah finished her sentence. "I'm going to be okay Mom, you don't have to worry," he reassured her.

"So, what do you want for dinner, sugar booger?" she said. Josiah grinned and looked at her with a knowing look that only a mom could interpret.

"Okay. Okay. We can go to Leo's Pizza." His mom said.

She knew that was his favorite restaurant, and after all, they didn't have too many options since they lived in the country outside of a small town. Josiah loved Leo's, and his mom was happy to accommodate.

The restaurant had been there for years. It was nearly a historical landmark. There was an Italian flag painted on the entire side of the small brick building, which was located on the corner of their downtown square. Like most small towns, the square had seen better days; times when the brick streets were filled with kids heading to Woolworth's drug store for an ice cream float, or families migrating to the small park in the middle of the square where they used to do summer concerts.

A large family originally from Italy started Leo's years before. They sometimes would call Josiah's mom "daughter" since her grandparents were from Italy too. But, as far as they knew, they weren't related. But it did have a way of making them feel welcome every time they dropped by. In a small town, everyone knows everyone's name. People who live in big cities don't get to experience this type of thing as much.

Leo's advertised that they made the best calzones in the world. While Josiah wasn't a world traveler, and couldn't verify their claim, he was inclined to agree. For dessert, he and his mom would always share a chocolate cannoli. She would get a mug of hot coffee, and he would get a tall glass of milk. Sometimes, not often, his mom would let him get a bottle of root beer.

Later that evening, after they got home from their Italian feast, Josiah's mom came into his room to say goodnight. She talked him through some of the details of their move and reminded him about the drive-in movie, not that she would ever think that he would forget, but because she wanted to end the day on a positive note.

"I've taken tomorrow off so I can get us packed. When you get home from school, you can help me get your room together," she said.

Josiah nodded. She sat on his bed and leaned over and kissed his forehead.

"Do you know how much I love you kid?" she asked.

"Too much," Josiah answered.

His mom smiled.

"I love you too much too," Josiah said as he sat up to give her a hug.

"Get some good sleep. We've got a busy couple of days ahead of us. And then we've got the movie Saturday night."

The movie idea turned out to be a great way to balance out the disappointment and drudgery of moving. As Josiah lay in bed, he experienced a mental tug of war as his thoughts drifted back and forth between the new dragon movie, and the fact that he only had two nights left in their house. He didn't want to fall to sleep being sad, so he decided to focus on the movie, which proved to be a successful strategy.

Chapter Five

The Midnight Conversation

Josiah had barely closed his eyes when he heard a pecking at his window again. *It could be the scary owl from the previous night*, he thought. At first he tried to ignore it, but it just got louder. He didn't want the sound to wake his mom so he rolled out of bed and crawled over to the window pane.

He tried to see what was causing the noise, but you know how hard it can be to focus on something right when you wake up. He decided to open the window to get a better view. He hoped he wouldn't find the mean owl.

As soon as he pushed the window up, he looked back down and saw not one, but three owls. He fell back onto the floor, but caught himself so as to avoid getting hurt and also to keep from making too much noise. He backed a few feet away from the window, unsure of what would happen next.

"Top of the evening to you," Gilbert said. Gilbert was the owl Josiah met earlier in the week. He had on the same clothing and eyeglass as before. "Mind to give me my cane back, my good boy? I'm assuming you still have it?"

Josiah knew he must be dreaming. Maybe that's why he was responding so routinely, as if it was it was perfectly normal for him to talk to an owl who was wearing clothes, an eye glass, and asking for his cane back. He walked over to his bed and pulled the cane out from under his pillow where he had placed it earlier.

"Many thanks, lad" Gilbert said.

"Now then," said another owl. This owl was shorter than Gilbert, and had bushy eyebrows. It wore circle shaped thick black-rimmed glasses and spoke with a similar accent. It looked like a more serious owl than Gilbert, but still friendly; not like the owl from the other night. The owl studied Josiah for a few moments.

"Name's Clive. At your service," the owl finally said with what looked like a smile, if owls can look like they are smiling.

"It is a pleasure to make your acquaintance," said another owl with a thick accented voice. "The name is Dorothy."

This owl looked like she was the same kind of owl as Gilbert and Clive, but her feathers were better groomed. She wore a large piece of jewelry, what adults call a "broach." She stood, or perched I suppose, in a more formal way and looked as though as she meant what she said: that she was truly pleased to meet Josiah.

Josiah sat up a little straighter, the way a young boy should instinctively act when being in the presence of a proper lady. But if his posture was more composed, his words certainly weren't. He couldn't quite think of what to say.

"Uh... I... ummm..." Josiah searched for words.

He was beginning to think this might not be a dream and that the owls might be real, which made him both excited and nervous, all at the same time.

"Don't be frightened dear," Dorothy said. "We're here to help you."

"To... to help? You're here to help me?" Josiah finally mustered up the certitude a complete sentence.

"Why, yes. Yes, my boy. We're here to help," Gilbert said with a sense of profound joy, as if their presence was one of the jolliest facts in the entire universe. And for Josiah, it actually was. But he was still trying to figure out if he was awake or dreaming. His eyes glossed over as he contemplated the situation at hand.

"Well?" Clive said.

Josiah just stared.

"Well?" Dorothy added.

"Huh?" Josiah said with a rather dumbfounded look.

His words had become a scarce commodity. He didn't mean to be disrespectful but he felt as though he was playing Scrabble® with a limited number of pieces.

"Huh" was the best he could do at the present moment.

"Dear boy, do you not understand us? We are here to help you."

"Um... with what?" Josiah responded. He should have immediately thought of the move, but he couldn't think of much of anything at the moment, other than simply being confounded at the idea of talking owls.

"Your problem," Clive added, "we have come to help you with your dilemma."

"My what?" Josiah said.

"A dilemma, dear," said Dorothy, "is a choice between two options. And you, my dear, have a dilemma. And we have come to help you in making your decision."

Josiah just stared back at her, not sure what to think.

Gilbert moved over on the branch and switched his cane to his opposite wing. Clearing his throat, he said, "Lad, your present situation is of utmost importance. And we have come to help you sort out what you should do."

And then it clicked. Josiah realized that they must be there to help him figure out how to save their farm. A look of excitement came over his face. His eyes lit up.

He leaned out the window and whispered, "Shhh. I don't want to wake my mom. I'll be right out."

Josiah put a sweatshirt over his pajamas and slipped on an old pair of tennis shoes. He grabbed the blanket that his mom always put on the foot of his bed, just in case he were to get cold during the night. He quietly made his way downstairs, being careful to skip over the third step from the bottom. He gently shut the front door behind him and quickly ran over to the tree outside of his window.

But when he got there, the owls were gone.

He scanned the surrounding trees, but saw nothing of the owls. After standing for a few seconds in silence, he began to hear voices. Their accents made it clear that it was the talking owls, but where had they gone?

"Over here, lad," Clive called out.

The owls had perched on a fence that framed the yard around Josiah's house. They were facing away from Josiah, looking out across their farmland on the right and the highway to the left. Josiah sat on a large boulder near the fence. He wrapped the blanket around him to keep warm, and leaned forward in anticipation of what the owls were going to say.

There was a full moon that night that looked like it was sitting on top of the trees at the far end of their field. Josiah simply watched the silhouetted owls perched on the wooden fence and listened to their conversation. He couldn't make out what they were entirely saying, but that was okay. Eventually they turned around.

Gilbert spoke first, "My boy, it seems you have come to a fork in the road."

"A fork?" Josiah said with a puzzled voice.

"Yes, a fork," Clive chimed in, "Not a real fork, mind you. You've come to a point of decision and you must go one way or the other."

Josiah was glad that Clive had offered a clarification. He would hate to think the owls had come simply to talk to him about forks. Josiah felt like he understood the reason they had come. It must be about their move. He was certain that was the reason they were there.

"So, what's the plan?" Josiah asked.

"Well, dear boy," Dorothy said, "our plan is to talk the thing out with you."

"About how we can save the farm?" Josiah said.

"Well, my boy," Gilbert spoke now, "we have not come to talk to you about saving the farm."

Josiah scooted back a little bit on the boulder and looked surprised. He said nothing.

Gilbert continued, "We have come for something much more important."

It was quiet for a little while. Josiah couldn't imagine what would be more important than saving their farm. He began to rethink the whole situation. Why else would these talking owls visit his window? What were they there to do?

Just then Josiah heard a loud shriek above his head. He looked up and saw the shape of another owl sitting on the branch of a tree that stretched out over the fence. The noise the owl made didn't sound pleasant. Then Josiah realized that this was the owl from the other night. It was a different kind of owl than the talking ones.

The shrieking owl still appeared to be mean. In fact, it even seemed scarier than it did the other night, especially since Josiah couldn't just quickly shut the window and keep it away. He was completely exposed sitting on the rock. And he wasn't totally convinced yet that the other owls might not be mean too. After all, maybe they had intentionally wooed him outside to bring him to the scary owl. Maybe this was a cruel trick.

He quickly got off the rock and picked up a stick from the ground and prepared to bat it away if it came close. Just then it launched off of its branch and swooped down towards Josiah, but before it came in reach where he might hit it, it turned and flew across the field towards the trees at the perimeter of their farmland. The other owls let out loud shrieks as it flew away. Josiah had never heard anything like that before.

At this point Josiah had gone around to the back of the boulder on the opposite side of the owls. He crouched down with his blanket draped across his shoulders, holding the stick he had picked up to defend himself. What did these owls want from him? Was this a nightmare? Would he wake up soon?

Just then Dorothy hopped from the fence to the boulder. She peered down at him with a motherly look that somewhat helped to stay his fears. He leaned back and looked up at her, as she leaned forward to look down at him.

"Are you mean like the other owl?" Josiah asked.

He should know that this was a direct question, and not very polite at that, but it seemed that the best way to find out was simply to ask.

Dorothy hopped down to the ground with a swoosh. "Who?" she said.

Josiah didn't know if she was asking a question or

just making the noise that owls normally make. "The owl that just flew away. Are you mean like that owl?"

"Oh, he isn't mean at all." Dorothy replied.

"He sure seems mean," Josiah said.

"He's just shy. His name is Reuel. He doesn't talk much, but when he does, it is always something important. He prefers to write or draw his messages," Dorothy said.

"Don't let Reuel bother you, my boy, should he feel as though he has a message for you he will find a way to let you know," Dorothy said as she made her way back to the fence. She nodded her head as if to direct Josiah to come up off the ground.

Josiah climbed back on top of the boulder leaving the stick behind him on the ground. He wrapped his blanket back around him and tried to get comfortable. The wind was picking up and he was starting to get a little cold. The owls had all turned around on the fence and faced Josiah on the boulder.

Gilbert asked Josiah a question that helped him realize what sort of problem they had come to help with, "Josiah, do you believe that nature is all there is?"

Josiah thought for a few moments but didn't respond.

Finally he asked, "Is that why you came? Because of what my science teacher said the other day?"

"Yes, dear," Dorothy said, "we have come because this is one of the most important questions you can consider. Your answer to this single question will have a profound impact on the rest of your life."

"It will?" Josiah said.

Clive spread his wings, which apparently he had not considered all of the implications of this move as it nearly knocked Dorothy and Gilbert off of the fence. They politely scooted over to give him more room.

"Eh, hem." Clive cleared his throat. "Everything you can see is not all there is, my lad," he told Josiah. "There is much more to your world than anything you can see with your eyes."

Clive swayed his head from side to side, the way owls like to do. He paused for a moment looking at Josiah.

"Look at the night sky and all of the stars," Clive said. "Do you truly believe that this is all there is?"

"No." Josiah answered. "There are a lot more stars that we can't see," Josiah said with a look of excitement. "My dad used to set up a telescope on clear nights and we would look at the stars and at the craters in the moon. He would always tell me that there were all kinds of stars and planets that we couldn't even see with our telescope."

"So what is beyond the stars?" Clive asked.

"Beyond the stars? More and more stars, I suppose," Josiah said.

"Do you think space goes on forever?" Clive asked.

"I don't know. I'm not sure. I guess I've never thought about it like that. I imagine it must," Josiah responded.

"What if it doesn't?" Clive asked trying to help the boy understand his point.

"Doesn't what?" Josiah said.

"Pay attention boy, this is very important," Clive said back, which made Josiah sit up.

"What if space doesn't go on forever?" Clive asked.

"Um... I'm not sure," Josiah said. "What could possibly be beyond space?"

Gilbert sat his wing on Clive's back letting him know he wanted to insert something into the conversation. Clive looked over with what could be interpreted as a little bit of annoyance, but he let Gilbert proceed.

"Lad, there are some important things you apparently haven't thought about before that we want to discuss with you. When your science teacher said that nature is all there is, what did you think about that?"

"I don't know. I don't know what else there could be but nature. And my teacher is really smart, so I guess he must be right," Josiah said.

"Do you think smart people have ever been wrong before?" Dorothy asked.

"Well, I'm sure they have. Nobody's perfect," Josiah answered.

Gilbert resumed talking, "Josiah, I want to help you understand something. There are a lot of people who think nature is all that there is, but this is simply wrong."

"It's rubbish," Clive added quite sternly. "It's simply rubbish." He waved his wings as he said this, but Dorothy and Gilbert moved out of the way in time. It was clear Clive felt strongly about this point.

Josiah tried to take it all in. *Talking owls had come to tell him that his substitute science teacher was wrong*, he thought to himself. To say this seemed odd to Josiah would be an understatement. He kept his skepticism silent as he listened to the owls talk about nature. Finally he couldn't contain his thoughts.

"So you guys are just here to tell me that my teacher is wrong about nature?" Josiah said with a tone of accusation. "Why wouldn't you come to help me with our farm? We are going to lose it, don't you know?"

"Dear, dear, we understand that, but we need you to understand that this is more important," Dorothy said with an empathic sound in her voice.

"I don't see how anything else could be more important than me losing my home," Josiah said.

It was much later at night than he normally was awake, and he wasn't even sure he was awake to begin with, and he was starting to become a little irritable. He was nearly always respectful to his elders, and it is not that he wouldn't have paid the same respect to the owls, they certainly seemed to be older, but he was sleepy and a little scared.

Clive gave a flap of his wings as he hopped from the fence to the boulder. He put his right wing on Josiah's arm and looked forward. This had a strange calming effect upon Josiah. The other owls quickly joined him.

"My boy, let me try to explain this to you. You live in world that you experience through your physical senses. In your world it is easy to believe that this is all that exists. It makes perfect sense that many people believe that the natural world is all there is. So much of what you learn in school is simply focused on observations of this world, and what you can experience through your senses."

"You mean your five senses: sight, touch, sound, smell, and taste?" Josiah asked. They had just talked about the five senses at school.

"Precisely," Clive said.

"Well, that makes sense to me," Josiah said.

"Nice pun, my boy," Gilbert chuckled.

Clive continued, a bit irritated about the whimsy of his colleague, "But there is more. You have other senses that are not based on what you can see and touch."

"Like what?" Josiah asked.

"In addition to your basic senses that you use every-day, there are other senses that you probably don't think about," Clive said.

"Like what?" Josiah said with his eyebrows raised.

"Like your sense of love and your sense of right and wrong. These are clues about the universe that tell us that there is more to our world than merely nature," Clive explained.

Josiah liked the idea of clues. He always enjoyed stories where you have to use clues to figure out a mystery. But he wasn't sure he fully understood what Clive was saying.

"Why are these clues so important that you came here to explain it to me? Is it really that big of a deal if I just agree with my teacher?" he asked.

Gilbert responded, "My boy, it is tragically important."

Clive added, "Lad, if you believe that nature is all there is then that is all you will live for."

"I think I'm starting to understand," Josiah said.

Josiah was a smart kid. He was beginning to figure

out that this was a big issue, even if he didn't completely comprehend all of the implications of what the owls were trying to tell him.

The lateness of the hour was finally catching up to him. He slid off of the boulder and onto the ground. He rested his back against the large rock and the owls moved back to the fence where they could look down at Josiah as they continued their conversation.

Once they had all resituated and gotten comfortable, Dorothy began to talk.

"Dear Josiah," she said with a soft but serious voice, "this is the most important decision you can ever make because it will affect the way you see everything else. Many people decide that nature is all there is, but never stop long enough to think about what that would really mean."

Josiah had never thought about anything like this. He looked back up at the stars and considered Dorothy's question. She didn't seem to mind that he didn't answer right away. She was happy to afford him as much time as he wanted to think it over.

After a couple of minutes, she broke the silence and said, "Let me ask you a specific question that I think will help, 'Do you think nature cares about whether or not you are going to lose your family farm?'"

Josiah looked at her, then back up at the stars, as he thought through what she said.

After a few moments Gilbert added, "Josiah, as I watch you sitting there staring up at the stars a thought occurred to me. Do you think the stars are up there looking down at you?"

"No. They couldn't be," Josiah said rather confidently.

"You are right lad, you can look at them but they cannot look at you. You can think about them but they cannot think about you. That is how it is with nature. In the grand scheme of things nature pays little attention to what is going with human affairs."

"I guess I haven't thought about it like that before. But if there is something more than nature then how do I know it cares?"

"That is a delightful question, my boy," Gilbert added.

"Insightful!" Clive inserted. "Nature is not something personal or rational."

"Rational?" Josiah interrupted.

"Yes, rational," Gilbert responded. "Nature does not have a mind. It does not think. Nature is not rational. Josiah, do you think nature has a mind or is able to think?" he asked.

"No," Josiah answered.

"Is that rock that you're leaning against personal?" Clive asked.

"No, I guess not," Josiah said.

"Well, does it have a personality? Is something like a person or completely different?"

"It's completely different than a person," Josiah answered.

"If nature isn't personal or rational, then why are you?" Clive asked.

"I don't know," Josiah said quietly.

It was clear he was thinking deeply about Clive's questions. He had never thought about this before.

Josiah looked up in the sky as he continued to think. He could make out the Big Dipper just overhead.

"How do you think humans can be personal and rational, if we are just a part of nature?" said Clive.

"I, I don't know. Um, I'm not sure," Josiah responded.

"Lad, I know this can be confusing, so let's just take it slow, " Clive explained. "If we are personal and rational, and if nature isn't either of those things, then it suggests that there is more to reality than just nature. In other words, nature is not all there is."

"I think I understand," Josiah said, still looking up.

Gilbert turned toward Clive with what looked like a pleased expression and added, "Josiah, it's not just the rock you are sitting on, or the stars that you are looking at that are not personal or rational. The same is true for the rest of the natural world for that matter. The universe isn't personal or rational. It doesn't have a mind. And if nature is all there is, then it certainly isn't interested in us or in the conversation we are sharing tonight."

"The universe doesn't care," Josiah repeated with a look of concern.

"No, dear, the universe doesn't care," Dorothy said with a hopeful tone that didn't seem to match her words.

"But my mom cares, and Addi cares. And her parents care. They care that we are losing our farm. They're letting us move in with them. They do care!" Josiah said, becoming defensive.

"Oh, dear, dear Josiah. You are absolutely right. Yes

they do care," Gilbert said. He looked down at Josiah with compassion. "Make no doubt, they do care deeply."

"That is one of the clues of the universe!" Clive added with excitement.

"There is something about you, and your mom, and Addi, and all humans for that matter, that is not merely part of nature. It is a clue to help you understand that there is more to life than nature. And if there is more, then wouldn't it be a pity, and really more than a pity, to live for this world when there is something else, something bigger and more grand?"

Josiah started to quietly cry. He was confused and the talk about the universe not caring was making him sad.

Dorothy hopped down to the ground next to Josiah and handed him a handkerchief. It was white with a red border and had a yellow eagle stitched into the corner. He dried the tears on his cheek, and without thinking, blew his nose into it. He sheepishly tried to hand it back to Dorothy, but she assured him that he could keep it.

"You need it more than I do," she insisted.

Josiah let out a small chuckle.

The other owls came to the ground as well to be closer to Josiah. He could tell they wanted to comfort him.

"Ever since my mom told me about the move, I was just hoping that somehow, someway, we wouldn't have to leave our home. I love it here. It reminds me of my dad. It's all I have left of him. And now it seems hopeless."

"My boy, hope is a good thing," Gilbert said. "You can't let go of it. It can give you strength when you need it most. But you must understand where hope comes from."

Clive chimed in, "It certainly doesn't come from nature, if nature is all there is."

Gilbert shot Clive a look as if his timing wasn't helpful. Clive shrugged his wings and looked away as he cleared his throat.

"Dear, dear, hope is good, but we cannot hope in nature if nature doesn't care. But if there is something more than just nature, then we can do even more than hope," Dorothy added, trying to be a bit more empathetic than Clive.

"Like what?" Josiah said as he worked hard not to sniffle. He had stopped crying but you know how your voice can become shaky when you are upset or worried.

Clive spread his wings apart again. This seemed to be something he did when he was excited. He accidentally whacked Gilbert on the side of the head, but Gilbert didn't seem to mind.

"Sorry, mate," he said.

"No worries," Gilbert said as he scooted out of range.

"Josiah, you have the wonderful opportunity to bring your concerns to the Ultimate Reality that is beyond nature," Clive said. "Nature may not be personal or rational, but what is beyond nature is certainly both."

Josiah looked at him as if things were beginning to become more clear.

"Oh, you mean, like God?" he asked.

"Yes, my boy. Yes! It is God!" Clive said. "He is what is beyond nature. And He is personal and loving and He knows all things."

"He knows everything?" Josiah asked. Josiah had been to church a few times in his life, not often, but the idea of God was not an entirely foreign concept to him. He had never really thought too much about what religion might have to do with real life, though.

"So if nature is not all there is, and if God is personal, then...," Josiah said, thinking out loud, "... then I can tell Him. Maybe He can help."

"He certainly can help," Dorothy added. "But look at me closely dear, His help doesn't always look exactly like we expect, or the way we might want it to look."

"It doesn't?" Josiah asked.

"No dear one, He knows far more about every situation than we ever will. And He cares deeply about us. He wants to hear our needs and worries. And He will do what's best," Dorothy added.

"Prayer is how we talk to God." Clive added.

"Talk to God?" Josiah said. He had never really thought of prayer as talking. It seemed more like a formal speech, or something you memorize and recite.

"Yes, when we pray we are able to express to God what concerns us most and He is able to work in us and through us to do what is best. When you pray you will begin to sense that there is a higher power at work in the universe than just nature and that this power is God. And He cares for you," Clive explained.

"So, does prayer change God," Josiah asked.

"No, dear boy, it changes us," Clive said. "It helps us to have peace, and sometimes it helps us to better understand God's plans for our lives, even the things we don't like. Prayer allows us to know God is in control and that He will work all things together for good."

These were some of the final words Josiah remembers clearly from his conversation with the owls, though much more was said. They talked for quite a while longer about God and how He isn't part of nature, but rather the Creator of nature. They talked about how He is in control of everything that happens.

There were many more things he discussed with the owls late into the night, until Josiah's sleepiness finally overtook him and it became difficult to keep his eyes open. As he drifted into sleep, one of the final things he saw was the silhouetted image of Reuel, the scary owl, flying overhead. He heard the same loud screech that he heard the other night and he woke up immediately. He wasn't outside anymore. He was now tucked warmly in his bed and it wasn't actually a screech, but his alarm clock going off next to his head. He sat up and looked towards the window, which was closed.

Chapter Six

Josiah Takes a Stand

As he got ready for school that morning, Josiah had no idea what to think. Were the owls just apart of his dreams again?

Even if they were just a dream, he had a renewed sense of hope about things. If there was more than nature, if God cared, then his situation might not be as bad as it seemed. Maybe there was a purpose. Even if it was a dream, perhaps it was an important dream to teach him an important lesson.

His mom pressed his door open and peeked inside to make sure he was awake. "Everything okay, sugar booger?" she said.

"Yep. Everything is awesome," he responded.

"Awesome, huh? I guess you're excited about the movie tomorrow night?

Josiah just smiled. He was excited about the movie, that was for certain, but there was something else. He didn't know quite how to explain it, and he didn't think it was a good time to tell her about the owls. He would save that for Addi on their ride to school.

After breakfast Josiah made his way to the bus stop. As soon as he opened the front door he saw that Addi was just making her way up the gravel road. He ran out and joined her.

On the bus he told her everything about the night before. They both gleamed with excitement as their minds raced back to their earlier conversation about the first time Josiah met Gilbert, earlier in the week. They still weren't sure if the owls were real, or just a dream. They didn't seem to mind. Even if the owls were only a part of Josiah's dreams, they certainly were exciting.

Eventually the conversation hit that inevitable awkward moment when no one really knows just what to say next. To break the silence, Josiah looked at Addi and asked, "So how are your talking squirrels?" She laughed. And then she punched him on the arm.

Before the bus made it to school she looked at Josiah with a more serious expression and asked him if he believed that there was more to the world than just nature; if he believed that there is a God who knows us and cares about us. But before Josiah could answer the bus driver bellowed out, "We're here. Time to get off the bus!"

Josiah looked at Addi and asked, "Why does he always say that?"

They made their way down the bus steps and headed into school. The bus had been running a little behind that morning so they had to hustle to make it to their lockers and then head off to class. Later that day at lunch they resumed their discussion in the cafeteria.

Josiah's mom hadn't been grocery shopping because of their upcoming move, so she had given him money to buy lunch at school. As they walked into the cafeteria Josiah saw a student carrying a tray with a pile of thinly sliced pieces of liver covered in onions situated next to a heap of green beans. He looked at Addi with his big brown puppy dog eyes, the kind of look you give when you need something, and she just laughed and said, "I'll share my sandwich with you."

They sat down at their usual table and split Addi's PB&J without the J sandwich. They didn't get to talk too much about the owls though. Their friends were sitting with them and they really didn't want to risk being laughed at if they were overheard speaking of talking owls.

Josiah used his lunch money to buy a candy bar from the vending machine, which he split with Addi, but before they could finish eating it, the bell rang. They finished the rest of the candy bar on the way to class.

The next couple of hours were rather humdrum but that all changed when they walked into their last class of the day. Their substitute teacher, Sam, let them know that their regular teacher, Mrs. Chesterton, would be back with them on Monday. He said that she and her baby were doing well and that she was looking forward to seeing them all next week.

"Since this is the last lesson I will get to give you guys, I thought I would end by returning to something we talked about earlier in the week," Sam said. "Because I think it is really important. Some of you weren't sure what to think about the statement that nature is all there is, or ever was, or ever will be. This is important because it really will affect the way you approach science."

Josiah felt a little uneasy. The owls had told him this was important too. But they were convinced that there is more to the world than just nature. And Josiah was inclined to agree with them.

It was almost as if he could hear Clive's voice in his ear saying, "Lad, if you believe that nature is all there is then that is all you will live for. But if there is more, then wouldn't it be a pity, and really more than a pity, to live for this world when there is something else, something bigger and more grand?"

His mind drifted back to the long conversation he had with the owls. A lot of what they said made sense to him. He started to chuckle when he thought of Clive accidentally hitting Gilbert in the head with his wing.

Sam had noticed that Josiah seemed distracted. When Josiah giggled at the thought of Clive, Sam politely asked him what was so funny.

"Oh, um, nothing," Josiah said. "Sorry, I didn't mean to laugh out loud."

But it was too late. Sometimes when you get a

teacher's attention, however you get their attention, you end up in the hot seat. It's not that Josiah was in trouble, but his teacher wasn't finished asking him questions.

"So, Josiah, what do you think about it?"

"About what?"

"About the statement that nature is all there is."

Josiah squirmed in his seat. He really didn't want to answer in front of everyone. But after talking to the owls, he felt like he was ready to give an answer.

But what would the owls say... he thought to himself for a moment to collect his thoughts.

"Do you have anything you want to add, Josiah?" his teacher asked.

"Um... yes... yes sir. Yes, I do have something I'd like to say," Josiah said a little shyly. He'd never really disagreed with a teacher in class before, so this was new ground.

"So, what do you think?" Sam asked.

Josiah could tell that his teacher really wanted his opinion, so he didn't feel too intimidated. He was just nervous that he might say something that would make his classmates laugh. And he definitely wanted to make sure he didn't let anything slip about the owls.

"I think there is more than just the stars," Josiah said.

"Yes, you're right Josiah. There are more than just stars. There's a lot more in the universe than just stars."

"Well, I mean that beyond the stars there is more, past any stars that we can see."

"That's right," his teacher said.

"But I don't just mean more space. What I mean is, well, that there are clues that tell us that nature is not all there is," Josiah responded.

"Josiah, science is able to tell us a lot about our world. For example, we can tell that the edge of our universe is moving outwards away from us, which tells us our world is expanding. This is evidence of what scientists call the Big Bang, when the world came into existence."

Josiah was truly curious, and so was the rest of the class. He was trying to make sense of what Sam was saying and see if it fit with what the owls had told him the night before. Maybe they were saying the same thing.

"So what made it come into existence?" Josiah asked.

"We don't really know for sure, but there are a lot of theories. Like I said the other day, some people think the universe came out of nothing," Sam said.

That certainly didn't make sense to Josiah. And the idea that the universe came out of nothing didn't seem to fit at all with what the owls had told him about God.

"Or what if maybe God made it?" Josiah said.

"That is a really good question, Josiah. Now we are touching on the importance of the statement that nature is all there is. Some people use God as an excuse to avoid looking for scientific answers," Sam said.

"But what if it is the answer?" Josiah asked.

"The answer to what question?" Sam said.

"To where nature came from. What if it came from God?" Josiah responded.

"Well, if nature is all there is then that means

there isn't something outside of nature like a god." Sam explained.

"But you said we can't see beyond the universe," Josiah said.

Sam tried to explain his logic to Josiah. "That's right we can't, but we know that nature is all there is, so if we could see beyond our universe, we would simply find more nature."

He was a good teacher, so he didn't want to simply speak over the students' heads.

Just then Josiah remembered how Clive had told him that there are clues to understanding our universe, things like love and the understanding between right and wrong that seem to be more than just nature. Something else that Clive said came to mind as well, that nature is not personal or rational. Josiah was still trying to make sense of this and so he simply asked his teacher.

"Is nature personal or rational?" Josiah asked.

Sam looked really surprised at this question. "Wow. Josiah that is a really insightful question." He continued to look with amazement at Josiah. "What made you think of it?" his teacher asked. Sam knew that Josiah had been really trying to understand this topic, it was clearly evident in his question.

"Well, um, (pause) someone (pause) told me recently that nature isn't all there is, that it makes more sense to believe that something, or someone, who is personal and rational created the universe. He, well they, meant God," Josiah answered.

Addi looked at him with a little bit of concern. They

made eye contact. They knew each other well enough that sometimes they could tell what the other was thinking just with a glance. It was as if Josiah's return look was his way of assuring her that he wasn't going to bring up the owls. Their entire class would think they were crazy.

"Josiah, if we believe that nature is all there is then we don't have to use God as an excuse," Sam explained.

"But I don't think it is an excuse," Josiah said back.

Sam turned away from Josiah and addressed the rest of the class. The last bell was about to ring and he wanted to bring some closure to their discussion. "Students, Josiah has brought up a really good point. And I don't think it would be entirely appropriate for me to say too much more about the matter. Josiah, thank you for your great questions. I hope everyone is able to think about this as much as you have," he said while looking back towards Josiah.

Just then the bell rang and everyone shot out of class as usual. Everyone except for Josiah and Addi, that is. But they didn't have much time to spare, since their bus driver, who was always in a hurry, wouldn't appreciate them being late.

"Thank you for teaching our class Mr. Sam," Josiah said. Even though the teacher had asked them all to call him by his first name, Josiah still wanted to be respectful.

"Thank you," Addi said.

"Oh, thank you guys. It has been a lot of fun. And I hope you both learned something. It has been a pleasure to be your teacher," Sam said.

Josiah asked a final question, "Mr. Sam, if nature is all there is... does the universe care about us?"

"Well, that is another good question, Josiah. I suppose that it doesn't," Sam answered.

"Josiah, we better hurry!" Addi interrupted as she tried to get Josiah to follow her into the hallway. She didn't want to miss the bus.

"Okay, okay. I'm coming," Josiah told her as he began to walk out of the classroom. "Thanks, Mr. Sam!"

"You bet, Josiah."

* * *

Josiah and Addi ran out to the bus and made their way to their normal seats with Josiah facing the window.

"I liked having Sam as a teacher," Addi said as she initiated their conversation for the ride home.

"Me, too," Josiah said. "I liked that he was willing to talk and he didn't seem to mind that I didn't agree with him."

"Yeah. That was pretty cool," Addi added.

"So, what are you guys going to do tonight?" Addi asked.

"We've got to pack. My mom took off work today so she could get most of our stuff boxed up. I've got to get my room ready when I get home," Josiah said.

"Do you want some help?" Addi asked. She was a thoughtful friend.

"That would be awesome," Josiah replied.

When the bus came to their stop they both hopped off and ran through Josiah's yard and up to his house. They could hear music playing as they lept up the front steps.

Josiah's mom loved music. Josiah's dad had an old record player, the kind with a handle on the side that you have to crank. She was playing some of his old big band records. You would have thought there was a live band playing in their living room the music was so loud. Old record players don't have a volume control, and with everything in boxes the music just seemed to bounce around their empty house.

"Mooom!" Josiah said in a loud voice trying to get her attention over the music.

His mom lifted the arm on the record player and the music stopped. The house instantly became quiet.

"Yes," she said turning towards him with a grin. "Why hello Addi," she said to Addi as Addi stepped inside. "Are you going to join us for pizza tonight?"

"Can I?" Addi asked.

"Yep. Your mom will be here soon and later your dad is going to bring pizza from Leo's."

A few minutes later Addis mom arrived. Josiah's mom wound up the record player and they all got to work, while the music again filled the home.

Josiah had a warm feeling deep inside that seemed to kind of feel like happiness, but a profound happiness that he would later understand as joy. In an odd way, packing just seemed like fun with the music playing,

Addi and her mom helping, and pizza from Leo's on the way. But it was even more than that. I think his joy was a result of growing to understand that there is more than nature, and that things happen for a purpose.

They were nearly finished with Josiah's room when Addi's dad finally pulled up in his police car with two pizza boxes. There are a lot of advantages to living in the country, but one disadvantage is that pizza places won't deliver. And by the time you drive into town and get the pizza, it can get cold and soggy by the time you get back home. So they usually would stick it in the oven for a few minutes and heat it back up. Addi's dad must have driven fast though, because the pizzas were still hot.

They all sat on the front porch and ate their pizza from paper plates. Addi's dad brought root beer from Leo's, which they drank straight from the bottles. It was a fitting feast for their last night on the family farm. It certainly should not have been a happy occasion, but there was a sweetness they all enjoyed just in being together. Even in the midst of their disappointment, there was a sense that everything was going to be okay. I'm not sure anyone could have explained it, even if they tried.

Addi and her parents stayed until late that evening when all the work was done. They stood on the front porch and discussed their plans for the following day. First thing in the morning Josiah and his mom would head to Addi's house for breakfast. Addi's father had borrowed a truck to move their boxes. After breakfast they would spend the morning getting everything moved over. And later in the day they would all head to the drive-in theater.

They said their goodbyes. Addi's mom and Josiah's mom gave each other a big hug and stood on the front porch holding each other for a couple of minutes. Josiah could tell they were both crying, but it wasn't an overly sad cry. It wasn't a joyful cry either, the kind of tears you cry when you are really happy. It was somewhere in the middle. It was a mixture of thankfulness for their family friendship and recognition that tomorrow the move would actually happen. This was their last night in their home.

But providence was stirring. And the owls weren't finished with their work just yet. After Addi and her parents left, Josiah and his mom went inside. The house was a maze of boxes. It was as foreign to Josiah as if it were someone else's home. He had never seen it this empty before. The truth was it had not been this empty for decades, really not since it had first been built long before Josiah was even born. It had been filled his entire life. This didn't seem like the house he had always known, which was always filled with family, the smell of good food, and the sounds of laughter, music, and love.

Josiah and his mom sat on the steps that led upstairs. His mom got out a package of cookies and poured what was left of the milk into two plastic cups. She held her cup over towards Josiah and he knew that meant a toast. They tapped their cups against each other and she said, "Here's to what's next." Josiah just smiled as he tried to hold back a tear. He really didn't feel like crying but sometimes your tears don't really bother with what you want to do anyways.

"How are you doing sugar booger?"

"I'm alright," Josiah answered as he pulled his arms inside of his t-shirt. He was getting cold. Anytime he did that his mom would tell him to stop because she said it stretches the shirt. But she didn't get on to him this time. She just stepped off the stairs to get him a blanket.

"Are you sure," she asked.

"Yeah, I'm doing okay," Josiah said. "I don't want to move but I'm looking forward to us staying at Addi's house for a while. I think it will be fun."

Josiah's mom walked back to the steps and sat down. When she opened up the blanket a white handkerchief fell out. "I wonder where that came from," she said out loud, not really looking for a response. She set it down on the floor without giving it much more thought.

But Josiah knew exactly where it came from. Or at least he thought he did. It had to be Dorothy's handkerchief that she had given him last night. It had the same red border and emblem with the yellow eagle on it. He must have left it folded up in the blanket he had taken outside.

That morning when he woke up back in his bedroom with no memory of how he got there, he was tempted to think the whole conversation with the owls was only a dream. Perhaps an important dream, but still only a dream. But deep down he felt like it was more than a dream, and this was the kicker. To find the handkerchief from Dorothy with the unique emblem was enough to seal the deal. The owls were real. They had to be.

They both covered the legs with the blanket and Josiah leaned his head on his mom's shoulder to hide his grin. They sat for a long time not saying anything. Josiah's mom drew strength from how well Josiah was doing. Her greatest concern was not about losing the farm, but worrying about him. And he seemed to be doing well.

She finally stood up and led Josiah upstairs. He had nearly fallen asleep resting on her shoulder. She walked him into his room and tucked him in bed and kissed his forehead. When she left, Josiah sat up. He couldn't help but think of the owls.

He got down on the floor and crawled over to the window, which was open. A cool breeze was gently shaking the tree branches just outside. He went back to his bed to get his blanket and pillow. He set the pillow on the windowsill and wrapped up in the blanket. Leaning on the sill, he looked out across the farm.

He really wanted to see the owls again, but he almost felt guilty for not being content with finding the handkerchief, which was about as good of confirmation that they owls are real as he could expect. *How much can one boy ask for?* he thought to himself. As he sat there he began thinking about everything they had told him. And he thought about his substitute teacher, and their conversation in class.

He was doing a lot of thinking on this last night in the house, but after all, this was his thinking spot. He might as well get some good use out of it one more time.

And then he did it. He had never really talked to God before, but tonight, on the eve of their move, looking out across the land that had belonged to his family for years, Josiah began to pray. *If God exists, and there is more than just nature, then God must care*, he thought.

So Josiah thanked God for caring. And he thanked God for Addi and her family. And he thanked God for his mom. And he told God how much he misses his dad.

He really didn't know how else to pray, which was probably a good thing, because he just talked to God like he used to talk to his father or his grandfather. But after a while, his eyelids began to get heavy. As every young boy can tell you, praying at night can make you sleepy. Before he gave in to sleep though, he asked God to help him and his mom with their move.

His prayers turned into dreams and his dreams turned into morning. He was startled awake by a loud banging at their front door. His mom was already awake in her room down the hall, packing her bedding into a box. She called out "Coming!" and quickly made her way down the steps.

Please know, that nothing, and I mean nothing, could prepare her for what she was about to hear. But Josiah would not be nearly as surprised; grateful, but not surprised.

Chapter Seven

The Map and the Feather

Addi's mom let out a scream.

Josiah sat up and scampered over to his window. He could see Addi's dad's police car in the driveway but he couldn't see his mom since she was standing under the awning that covered their front door. Josiah made his way, as quickly as he could, down the stairs to see what was the matter.

He was surprised to find Addi, her mom and dad, and his mom all standing with their arms around each other in almost a huddle formation just inside the doorway. His mom turned around to welcome Josiah into the group and he could tell she was crying. She was sobbing, in fact. But the corners of her mouth, between sobs, curled upwards into a smile.

"What's wrong? What happened?" Josiah said with a mixture of excitement and concern.

"We don't have to move!" his mom said as she wrapped her arm around his side and bent down to one knee. "We don't have to move!" she said again.

Josiah, looking confused, turned to Addi's dad. The other evening when he first learned the news of the state taking possession of the family farm, Addi's dad had taken a leadership role in the conversation about their future. He naturally looked to him for an explanation of what was going on. He was thrilled to hear that they weren't moving, but extremely confused as to what was happening.

"Josiah," Addi's dad said, "it's true. You don't have to move."

Josiah looked relieved but still perplexed. But with news this good, he didn't want to be overly analytical. So, with a wide grin he joined the huddle and they all held each other as they wept and laughed.

After everyone calmed down a little, Josiah reasserted his question about what was going on. Everyone except Addi's dad sat down on their front steps. Josiah looked to Addi to see if she would give him an explanation.

"I don't know. Daddy just picked me and Mommy up from the house a couple of minutes ago. All he has said is that you guys don't have to move."

Josiah turned to Addi's mom but she was looking to her husband with tear filled eyes as she awaited an explanation like everyone else. Josiah's mom pulled Josiah close to her side as they listened to Addi's dad explain everything in detail.

Addi's father pulled out an envelope from his back pocket. He unfolded it and pulled out something that looked like old paper. It was brown from age and looked thicker than regular paper.

"I had heard rumors of this, but now I know it's true. And this changes everything!" He said with excitement. "I found it myself this morning!"

"What did you find?" Addi's mom asked.

Josiah's mom seemed a little disinterred in the details. She trusted Addi's dad and he said they didn't have to move, so she seemed content to bask in the good news.

Addi's mom, on the other hand, was insisting that he explain the whole thing.

"I found it earlier this morning," he told her.

"Well, I know you found it. You're holding it up for all of us to see," she said.

"Not this," he replied.

"Then what is it that you found?" she replied.

"I found the nest. I found it. And it's on your property," he said as he looked directly at Josiah.

Josiah was still confused, and so was everyone else it seemed. He couldn't imagine what the big deal would be with finding a nest or why that would have anything to do with them keeping their farm.

"It's an owl nest," Addi's dad said.

"Owl?" Josiah asked. He turned and looked to Addi with an expression of utter excitement. She shrugged her shoulders and grinned back.

"This morning when I came out to my car to do my

morning patrol through the state park down the street,
I found this stuck beneath my windshield wiper," he
explained. "And this is what was inside."

He held up the aged piece of paper from inside the
enveloped so everyone could see.

"I don't get it," his wife said. "What is it?"

"Well it seems like it's some kind of thin leather.
Some kind of animal skin that has been dried out so
you can write on it," he replied as he continued to
hold it out so everyone could study it.

"That's not what I meant," his wife continued. "What
is *on* it?"

"Well, I didn't recognize it at first either. It has a
different language on it, but this right here seems like
a key. The word *borealis* is written above the star."

"What's that mean?"

"Well, I'm still not totally sure. But Aurora Borealis
means 'northern lights.' They are lights you can see
in the summer sky if you live in the far north. So my
first guess was that it means north. And that's when
I realized than it's a map key."

Josiah reached his hand out and Addi's dad let him
take it for a closer look. It felt funny in Josiah's hand.
Her dad was right, it was some kind of leather. It was
smooth and thin.

"It does look like a map," Josiah said as he squinted
his eyes to try to make sense of the lines on the page.

"Wait a minute, that looks like the town," he said
with excitement.

"You're right Josiah," Addi's dad said, "and if you

follow the creek that runs through town, you will see..."

Josiah interrupted him, "Hey, that's our house!"

Everyone leaned in over Josiah to look at the map that he was holding on his lap. There was a crude circle around a portion of land in the vicinity of their family farm on the map with the word *nidus* written above it.

Addi's dad pointed his finger at the center of the circle and said, "And that's where I found the nest."

As he said this he walked over to his car and put his hand in the window and pulled out a feather. It was brown and white and the stem of the feather was stained black.

"This was with the envelope, and it looks like it's what was used to draw the map."

Addi reached up for the feather and her dad handed it to her. She held it up and looked closely at it. She turned towards Josiah with a knowing smile.

"When I first found the feather, I had a hunch," Addi's dad said.

"About what?" Josiah's mom asked.

"I've heard rumors about folks seeing a northern spotted owl around these parts recently. This looks a lot like one of their feathers, though I wasn't sure. But I knew for certain when I found the nest."

"Where did you find the nest?" his wife asked.

"Well, sort of. It's more like it found me. After I found the map under the windshield wiper, I decided to take the four-wheeler out to track down whatever the map was pointing to in the circled area. I made it to the general area, but I wasn't having any luck in figuring out what was supposed to be there. I circled around a few times, looking up into the trees, and then it hit me."

"You mean you figured out where the map was leading you to?" Josiah's mom asked.

"No. Not exactly. *It* hit me," he said.

"What hit you?" Addi asked.

"An owl hit me. Right on the side of the head. It knocked me off my four wheeler."

"Are you okay?" his wife asked.

"I'm fine. It didn't really hurt, it just startled me. What hurt most was when I landed. I fell right on top of what I thought was a stick, but it turned out to be a funny looking little wooden cane," he said as he rubbed his back.

"And when I looked up, the owl that knocked me off my four wheeler... it was flying away and I just caught a glimpse of it... but I could have sworn that it... well, it sounds crazy, but it looked like it was wearing clothes, like a little cape. I don't know. I think I must have hit my head pretty hard when I landed."

"I'm glad you're okay, but I'm not sure I understand how you finding the owl nest has anything to do with the interstate, and with us losing the farm," Josiah's mom said with concern.

"That's the thing. I thought the feather looked like it was from a northern spotted owl. But as I lay there on my back looking up I saw the nest inside the large oak tree, on the back half of your property. The one Josiah and Addi like to climb."

"I know that tree!" Addi and Josiah said in nearly perfect unison.

"I climbed up the tree and sure enough, there was a grown northern spotted owl sitting in the nest. It didn't even act scared. It just sat there and stared at me. It was amazing," Addi's dad said.

"So what is the big deal about northern spotted owls?" Josiah's mom inquired.

"They are classified as threatened animals in the United States. And you are not allowed to cut down any trees within a mile and a half radius of their nests," he said with excitement. "I've already called my supervisor and he's begun the work of having your property protected by the U.S. Fish and Wildlife Service due to hosting a threatened species."

Now it all made sense for Josiah's mom. But it made even more sense for Addi and Josiah. They knew a little more about these owls than the adults would have imagined.

Sometimes it feels like real life should have theme music like they do in the movies. If Josiah could have picked a song for the moment it would have been one of his dad's old records with big band music.

All of the conversation faded into background noise as Josiah's mind drifted away. That warm feeling started in his chest again, but this time it seemed to work its way out through his fingertips. His face might not have shown it, but on the inside he was grinning from ear to ear.

Addi's dad talked for quite a while longer about the

details of what they would need to do, and all of the implications of finding the nest of a northern spotted owl on their property. After they had talked at length about the owls, they started the process of unpacking all of the boxes and getting the house back to normal. Unpacking seemed to go a little faster than it did when they were packing up.

They ended the day just as they had planned, by going to the drive-in theater for the new dragon movie. They all sat on old blankets in front of Addi's mom's car that they had driven to the movie. Addi sat between her parents and Josiah snuggled up next to his mom.

They didn't have to say anything. They all knew they were blessed. From time to time Addi would lean forward and look over at Josiah and the two would smile.

This was one of Josiah's favorite days from all of his childhood.

The months that followed were filled with research teams and legal disputes between politicians and environmentalists. It seemed like pictures of Josiah's farm were on the newspaper with a new heading almost every other day.

But finally, just after Christmas, the old family farm was declared "off limits." That meant that Josiah and his mom wouldn't lose their house. And that meant that one day Josiah would inherit this land, just like his father had done, and his grandfather before him.

Through the years Josiah has told this story over and over again about how the owls saved his family farm. Inevitably, someone always makes some sort of comment about how great nature is. While Josiah never argues with them, deep down, he knows that there is something even greater than nature.

And for that he is profoundly grateful.

DISCUSSION GUIDE

EVERY PERSON HAS A WORLDVIEW AND EVERY WORLDVIEW IS A STORY. The secular worldview is based on a belief that the cosmos is all there is, or ever was, or ever will be. It's a story that started by chance, is governed by nothing, and is heading nowhere.

On the other hand, the Christian narrative begins with the belief summarized in John's gospel, "In the beginning was the Word . . . and the Word became flesh." The Christian story is simply better, and to borrow a pet phrase from Henry Kissinger, "it has the added advantage of being true."

This story of talking owls is intended to serve as a conversation starter; a place to begin a discussion about what best accounts for the human experience: Nature or God. Either nature is pointing inward, towards itself, or it is pointing outward to a loving and powerful Creator. As Clive said, there are clues that show us nature is not all that exists.

DOWNLOAD NOW

Download a discussion guide to supplement your reading of *The Owlings* by visiting theowlings.org/discussionguide.

Thank you for your support of this project. If you enjoyed The Owlings please help us spread the word, and consider visiting Amazon to leave a kind review. Stay tuned for more Owlings stories in the future, as these four talking owls, Gilbert, Clive, Dorothy, and Reuel, unpack fundamental concepts of a biblical worldview for readers young and old alike.

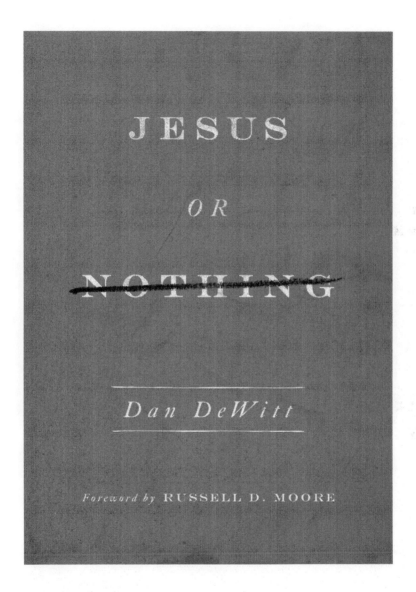

JESUS OR NOTHING

Dan DeWitt

Foreword by RUSSELL D. MOORE

JESUSORNOTHING.COM